T0132363

BOOK TWO

Goodnight Irene

Adventure in the still Of the Night

MONKEY BUSINESS

DEBBY HARRIS

Balboa Press books may be ordered through booksellers or by contacting:

Balboa Press
A Division of Hay House
1663 Liberty Drive
Bloomington, IN 47403
www.balboapress.com
844-682-1282

ISBN: 978-1-9822-5684-5 (sc)
ISBN: 978-1-9822-5685-2 (e)

Library of Congress Control Number: 2016916682

Print information available on the last page.

Balboa Press rev. date: 10/22/2020

BALBOA.PRESS

Goodnight IRENE
adventures in the still of the night
MONKEY BUSINESS

DEBBY HARRIS

Edited by: Tara Ann Colvin

"One, two, three, four, five, six, SEVEN!!!" Irene squealed with excitement as she finished counting the fireflies in her jar. "I caught seven light bugs, Aunt Millie!!" said Irene as she came skidding around the corner of the kitchen counter while Aunt Millie was finishing up the evening's dinner dishes. "Light bugs huh?" said Aunt Millie with her usual excepting smile and jolly voice. Irene quickly responded, "Well I know they are called fireflies but I like to call them Light Bugs because they light up!" "You can call them anything you like as long as you go back outside and let them out of your jar...I think I hear their mama calling them in for bedtime." Aunt Millie had a way of getting Irene to do the right thing without making her feel like she was hurting anyone. "Oh. Ok, I'll be right back" said Irene as she skipped back outside with her friends to say goodnight.

Irene came back into the kitchen where Aunt Millie was just putting the last dish away, the remaining scent of meat loaf, mashed potatoes and gravy and corn on the cob where still lingering. As Aunt Millie turned around, Irene's big, beautiful blue eyes grew even larger than usual and she got a giant smile on her face as she saw Aunt Millie holding a plate with fresh strawberry shortcake made with the strawberries she and Irene had picked from the garden that morning. "Now you enjoy the fruits of your labor, my dear." said Aunt Millie as she sat the plate down in front of Irene. "I will go and start your bath. "Irene took the first bite of her shortcake with the giant, juicy, red strawberries and homemade whipped cream.

Before she knew what happened, she had devoured the whole plate of desert and was in the bathroom waiting for the bath tub to finish filling with quite a bit of whipped cream and strawberry juice still on her lips. Irene loved this time of night. Most children aren't so excited to get ready to go to bed but Irene couldn't wait because she went on the most amazing adventures into the still of the night among the diamond scattered sky to another place.

And so it began.

Bath…………check

Jammies…...check

Brush teeth…check

Read a book…check

8pm bedtime...check

As Aunt Millie finished tucking Irene in her very cozy bed, you could almost feel the excitement in the air as Irene heard the familiar squeak of the wood floor and the click of the door closing. Irene snuggled up in her freshly laundered sheets that smelled like fresh lavender and pulled her trusted pal Oliver in close. Irene started her night in the usual way.

Goodnight sunshine...

Goodnight moon...

Off to dreamland...

I'll be back soon...

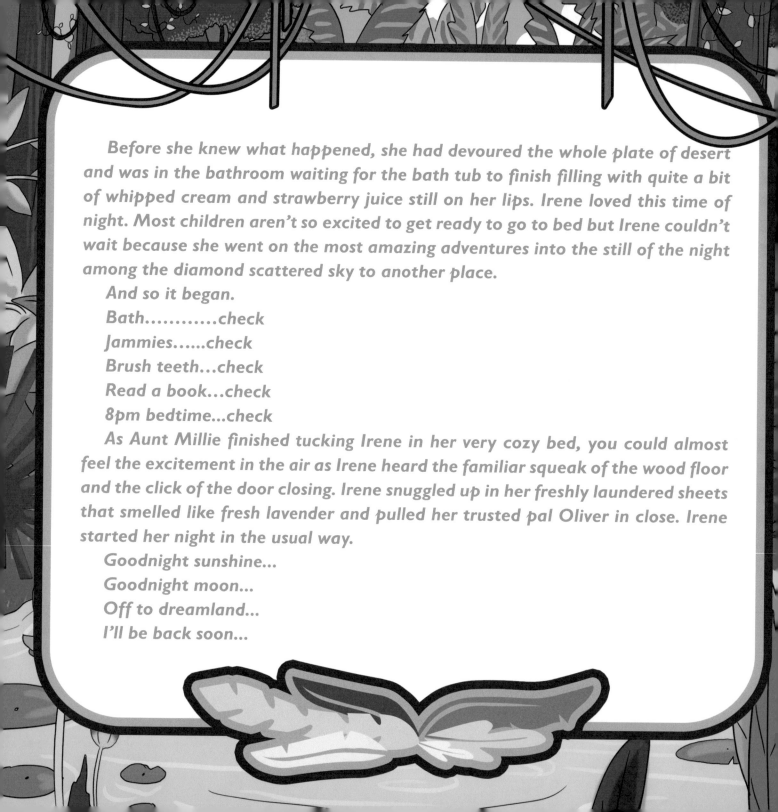

Irene's eyes grew heavy as she counted in her head how many "Light Bugs" she had caught that night. One, two, three, four, five…before she got to six Irene was fast asleep ….but not for long. A warm feather like breeze woke Irene to find herself sitting on the branch of an extremely tall tree. Before she could get startled at the sight of being up so high in the sky, she looked to her right and saw Oliver, her rather large pet owl who guides her on her adventures, which gave her a sense of comfort. His beautiful feathers of forest green and sunshine yellow shimmered as the sun peeked through the leaves of the majestic tree. "Nice view, isn't it" said Oliver in his wise but endearing voice. Irene looked around taking note of the many different trees and foliage below. So many vibrant colors. Like one of Aunt Millie's famous Rainbow Salads; lots of different greens with a scattering of other vegetables and fruit to bring it to life.

She saw so many beautiful flowers in the most amazing color combinations. Irene almost felt like she and Oliver had woken up in a watercolor painting. As Irene took in the heavenly view and enjoyed the calming breeze, she was suddenly shocked back into reality with the alarming sounds of what sounded like screaming coming from the ground below. As Irene flinched, Oliver gently curved is large and comforting wing around Irene to steady her. "What was that?" Irene said with an urgency in her voice. "What's going on down there?" "You are hearing the sounds of bullying." Said Oliver. "In case you didn't realize it, we have landed in the rainforest." Oliver continued. "Look in the distance…can you see the tops of those palm trees?" Irene looked intently across the sky to the tall grove of Palm trees and as she looked more intently, she said, "Who is up in those trees and what are they doing? " "They are monkeys and they're picking coconuts." Oliver said as if Irene should know this already. Continuing on, Oliver said, "The Native people of this region train these monkeys to climb the trees and bring the coconuts back to them." Irene thought that was a pretty smart thing to do since the monkeys could so easily climb the trees.

"So why did you say that I was hearing the sounds of bullying?" she said.

"Come, let's go a little closer and I will explain" said Oliver as he stood up, prompting Irene to hop on his back. "Where are we going now?" asked the ever inquisitive Irene. As Oliver took flight, he said, "I want to take you a bit further into the forest to where the monkeys live."

Irene jumped on Oliver's sturdy back as they flew through the beautiful forest, past some of the most amazing, colorful butterflies, flowers and trees. As Oliver flew, Irene felt like she was looking through a kaleidoscope. Before she knew it, Irene and Oliver were sitting once again in a tree overlooking the forest below only this time they weren't up quite so high and Irene could see below quite clearly. "It looks like the Monkeys are having some sort of meeting down there." Said Irene. "Yes, indeed they are." Said Oliver. "When I told you that you were hearing the sounds of bullying, I was speaking of one monkey in particular. He goes by the name of Max. Max is quite a bit bigger than the other monkeys.

When he and the other younger monkeys go out to do the climbing and picking, Max figured out that because he was bigger and stronger than the others, he could overpower the smaller monkeys and take the coconuts as his own without doing the work. One day, as they were doing their work, an Elder from the tribe watched as Max bullied his way through the day.

He also watched quietly as Max came back that night bragging about how many coconuts he had picked that afternoon. Later that evening, the Elder went to the Head of their tribe and told him what he had just witnessed." Oliver sat quietly for a moment as he could see that Irene was thinking about this story. "This reminds me of a kid I know at school" she began. "He is always bullying smaller kids around and making them give him their lunch money or snacks. He isn't very nice!" Irene was noticeably irritated by this story. Oliver said "Has he ever bothered you at school?" Irene sighed and said "No, but I have seen him in action and it bothers me!" "So, what do you think they're talking about down there?" Irene said inquisitively. " They are making a decision on what they should do about Max. Instead of just punishing him, they want him to learn from this." Oliver turned his ear in the direction of the group so he could listen more intently. All of the sudden Oliver and Irene see Max and the others coming back to their village.

"What's happening down there?" Irene can't wait to know what's going to happen next.

Oliver turned to Irene and said, "They have decided to send him to the Reflection Pond." "Reflection Pond?" said a confused Irene. "Yes, this is a pond that one is sent to when there is a problem like this. "Ok…." Said Irene, now more confused than ever.

Oliver continued," Sometimes it is better for the student to find his or her own answers instead of having someone give out a punishment that you can get through and then most likely forget what you were suppose to learn from it." Irene quickly said, "Student?" "Actually, Irene, we are all students in this life. There is always something for us to learn so that we can continue becoming a better, more compassionate being." Oliver continued. "Ok, so can you please explain the Reflection Pond?" she said with a very uneasy tone. "Of course," said Oliver, clearing his voice. "The student is sent to the pond and is told to stay there until he or she understands." "Understands?" Said Irene. "What I mean by that is the student is supposed to look into the pond at his or her reflection. At first, some are afraid of the reflection looking back at them because they have never seen themselves before and some get angry and aggressive thinking that another is staring at them." Irene sat looking a bit puzzled but soon looked back at Oliver saying, "What are they supposed to "understand" from looking into a pond?" "Awe…" said Oliver. "I've been

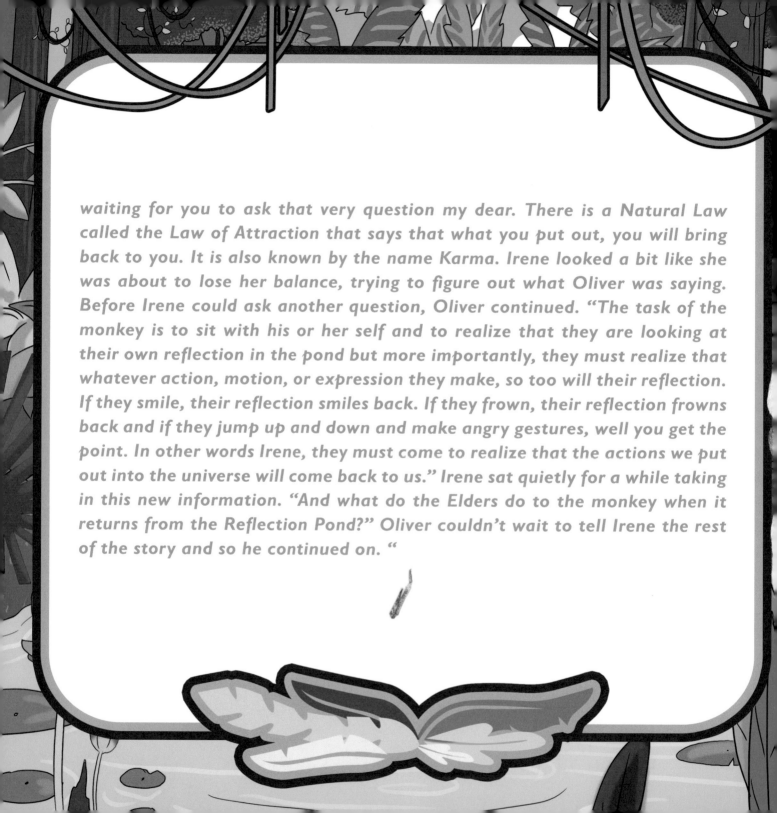

waiting for you to ask that very question my dear. There is a Natural Law called the Law of Attraction that says that what you put out, you will bring back to you. It is also known by the name Karma. Irene looked a bit like she was about to lose her balance, trying to figure out what Oliver was saying. Before Irene could ask another question, Oliver continued. "The task of the monkey is to sit with his or her self and to realize that they are looking at their own reflection in the pond but more importantly, they must realize that whatever action, motion, or expression they make, so too will their reflection. If they smile, their reflection smiles back. If they frown, their reflection frowns back and if they jump up and down and make angry gestures, well you get the point. In other words Irene, they must come to realize that the actions we put out into the universe will come back to us." Irene sat quietly for a while taking in this new information. "And what do the Elders do to the monkey when it returns from the Reflection Pond?" Oliver couldn't wait to tell Irene the rest of the story and so he continued on. "

This is the most incredible and I think the most beautiful part of the ritual. When the monkey comes back, the entire tribe joins in a large circle with the one who returned in the center and they spend the next few hours taking turns telling them all the good things about them and how important they are to the tribe and how they are an important piece of the puzzle that makes them all whole." Irene is mesmerized by this new information responding with the only thing that she can come up with which is "WOW!" Oliver could see that this had quite an impact on Irene . After a few moments of contemplation…Irene said, "I wish we had a Reflecting Pond at home because I can think of a lot of kids that could use it." "Oh, but you do." Said Oliver. "It is called a mirror." "Oh my gosh!! You're right!" Said Irene. "I forgot about the mirror." Irene got so excited about it that she lost her balance and started to fall off the tree branch but Oliver quickly swooped down and she landed gently on his back.

As Oliver flew in a circle over the tribe, Irene waved goodbye even though they weren't aware of their presence. Oliver landed in a beautiful clearing, surrounded by all the lush green trees and colorful flowers and found a soft spot to sit for a while. Irene was noticeably in deep thought over their encounter with the monkeys and the story about how they deal with bullying. "How do you think the mirror in your bathroom at home can be of help to you?" Oliver said to Irene prompting her to think deeper than usual. "Well," said Irene, "I understand the idea of looking into the mirror can be like the reflection pond and I understand what you are saying about the Law of Attraction, but I'm trying to figure out how I could let the other kids know about this." Oliver looked at Irene in his gentle way and before he could say anything, Irene said, "I've got it!"

I am supposed to do a report at school and have been trying to figure out what to do it on and this could be a great subject! I could bring in mirrors to demonstrate the idea of the reflection pond and then the students could take turns looking into the mirror to see how it works." "I think that could be a very good idea"." Said Oliver.

"Oh! And I have another idea!" Said Irene. "How about if I have everyone write a nice comment on a piece of paper and we put them in a hat and then we could all sit in a circle and take turns pulling them out of the hat and reading them out loud to each other?" "Well, that sounds like a great idea." Said Oliver beaming with pride. It always gave Oliver such a great feeling of satisfaction when he could see that his "student" had learned another valuable lesson. Oliver and Irene sat for a bit taking in all the beauty of the rain forest and the sounds of the exotic birds singing. Irene became so relaxed that she curled up next to her cozy friend Oliver and drifted off to sleep. Oliver sat with Irene curled up in his comforting wings as she slept, reflecting on their latest adventure. He was quite satisfied that Irene had grasped the concept of Karma and how our actions always cause a reaction. He knew that Irene's idea of using mirrors to explain the story of the reflection pond would be something the kids would remember and having them all say something positive about each other, out loud, would make everyone feel good.

Irene was sound asleep when she felt the soft hand of her Aunt Millie on her shoulder. As Aunt Millie started her usual morning ritual, saying:

"Wake up, wake up, it's time to say, thank you, thank you for another day." Irene's sleepy eyelids slowly opened to see Aunt Millie's sweet face and Irene smiled as she sat up and got a good morning hug. Aunt Millie's hugs were the best way to start the day. As Irene was getting ready for school, she couldn't help but to get excited about the report she would do and how she would tell the story of the reflection pond and hoping that it would make everyone in her class stop and think before they said anything negative to anyone. Just as Irene was heading out for school, she caught her own reflection in the mirror and she smiled and said to herself, "Today is going to be a great day!" And with that thought, Irene was off to school and looking forward to her next adventure.